HUGO
and the Ministry of Holidays

First published in 1980 by Andersen Press Ltd
and Hutchinson Group (Australia) Pty Ltd

Picturemac edition published 1986 by
Macmillan Children's Books
A division of Macmillan Publishers Limited
London and Basingstoke
Associated companies throughout the world

British Library Cataloguing in Publication Data

Ross, Tony
    Hugo and the Ministry of Holidays.
    I. Title
    823'.914[J]   PZ7

    ISBN 0-333-41981-2

Printed in Hong Kong

HUGO
and the Ministry
of Holidays

Tony Ross

MACMILLAN CHILDREN'S BOOKS

Hugo wanted a blackboard and easel.

He had always longed for one, ever since he was little, but they were too expensive.

Mother always said, "Wait until Christmas."

Hugo waited, and waited, and waited.

He was born in April, so Christmas seemed *such* a long way away.

But at last it was Christmas Eve, and Hugo carefully wrote a note to Santa, in big, neat letters:

"PLEASE MAY I HAVE A BLACKBOARD AND EASEL PLEASE.

      THANK YOU.

      HUGO."

Hugo lay awake that night wondering if Santa would find such a small letter, or would the wind blow it out of the chimney?

He thought how helpful a blackboard would be. He could learn to spell properly and write books, he could draw pictures ... and then he fell asleep.

It was still dark when Hugo woke, a frosty Christmas morning.

Jumping to the bottom of his bed, he grabbed the shape that lay there in the half light—a beautiful Easter egg!

"Catswhiskers!" gasped the disappointed mouse. "This *can't* be right. I'd better return it right away."

But *how* do you take a Christmas present back?

Pink lardermice know very well that Santas come down chimneys, so, pulling on his jersey, Hugo went to the fireplace. To his surprise he found a woollen scarf, knitted in coloured stripes, stretching up into the gloomy flue. As the scarf was knotted, Hugo decided that it was meant to be climbed. Gripping the Easter egg with his tail, the mouse clambered up into the dark.

The coloured scarf twisted out of the top of the chimney and wriggled away down the roof. It made a bridge down to the ground where it disappeared into a rabbit hole.

Hugo struggled on. It was dark in the rabbit hole and the snores of sleeping rabbits came from every direction.

"They must be dreaming of Christmas pudding," thought Hugo, as he followed the scarf.

The rabbit hole went to the top of a high hill, where the scarf looped upwards through the branches of a tall elm. From there it made another bridge to the nearest cloud.

Beyond the cloud, the scarf sloped down gently to the tip of the world. Lying on his tummy, the mouse slid faster and faster, his whiskers streaming out behind him. The only thing he could think about was how long it must have taken to knit the scarf.

After what seemed ages, Hugo landed with a BUMP in a pile of soft snow. The land was ice white, and he looked around him with a shiver.

In the distance, a white tower peeped over sugar and salt mountains, and as there was nowhere else to go, Hugo set off towards it.

"This must be the North Pole!" he gasped, as the wind clawed his jersey.

Hugo wiped the frost from a notice at the foot of the white tower. It read: MINISTRY OF HOLIDAYS.

There was no door, only a screen of soft snow that closed again once he had pushed through it.

It was quite warm inside, and Hugo found himself in a great hall, with stairs twisting off in every direction. Pieces of paper were scattered over the floor. Hugo looked at one of them: it was a letter to Santa.

All the staircases had signs on them, with arrows pointing upwards. One said BIRTHDAYS, another said SUMMER HOLIDAYS. The mouse went to the staircase marked THE MINISTER and began to climb.

The stairs led to a blue door that stood ajar. Hugo peeped into a cluttered office. An old man was trotting up and down, his arms full of letters. He wore red clothes and a green eyeshade.

"SANTA CLAUS!" shouted the mouse, rushing forward holding out his Easter egg.

"Oh NO!" screeched the old man, dropping his letters and clutching his beard. "Not *another* complaint?"

Hugo poured out his story. The old man jumped up and down.

"I'm only Santa Claus at this time of year you know!" he screeched. "All the rest of the time I'm seeing to birthdays and Easters and..."

He flopped down and sobbed, "There's just too much work to do!"

Hugo felt sorry for the old man. "Can I help?" he said.

"No one can help," sniffed Santa, wiping his eyes with his beard.

Taking Hugo by the elbow, he led him to a big brown curtain covering one wall. He swept the curtain aside, and the mouse found himself looking down on a vast room. In the middle, a computer chattered away madly, sending red tape streaming out onto the floor. Lots of Santas were running about, peering at the red tape, then scribbling addresses on Christmas boxes. It seemed that everyone had his own Santa. There were cat Santas, dog Santas, all sorts of animal Santas, even an elephant Santa. Easter Bunnies only added to the confusion, getting their squashy Easter eggs mixed up with everything.

Santa stared at the confusion. "It gets even worse when the busloads of fairies arrive, you know, the ones that put the money under the pillows when children lose their first teeth. They're *so* scatter-brained."

Hugo had been thinking. He had a plan and he *knew* it would work. "Why don't you get all the fathers and mothers to help?" he said. "You could start delivering presents in October, say, and leave them with the fathers or mothers. Then on Christmas Eve *they* could quite easily slip them into their own children's stockings. That way you wouldn't have to rush around on Christmas Eve yourself, and you'd have lots of time to read the letters and get the addresses right!"

Everybody thought it was the best idea in a thousand years.

The Under-Secretary for Dreams issued a special dream to one parent from each house in the world to come at once to the North Pole. As dream travel is very fast (much faster than a rocket ship), a great snoring crowd of snoozing parents was soon gathered around the Minister of Holidays.

Santa, in his dress uniform, and mounted on a reindeer, explained the change of plans. Everyone present nodded and seemed to understand (all except the Easter Bunnies, who understand very little).

When he had finished, Santa led Hugo away and the Under-Secretary made sure the parents all got home safely.

"Thank you so much, mouse," said Santa, when they were sitting together in his cosy flat at the top of the Ministry. "I feel a lot better about things now."

Santa told Hugo stories of past Christmases, while they ate Eskimo cake and sipped China tea. At last it was time for Hugo to go.

"The coloured scarf is rolled up for next year now," said Santa. "I'll call a dreamboat to take you."

He rang a little silver bell and a polar bear in an admiral's hat appeared at the door. Hugo's eyes felt heavy now, and he was carried out to where a funny little boat waited in the snow.

The last thing the mouse remembered was the polar bear shouting, "Cast off!" and the dreamboat sails filling with an icy wind that smelled of marshmallow.

He woke up with a jolt, sitting at the bottom of his bed. To his surprise he was still holding his Easter egg, as if his adventures had never happened at all. His bedroom clock showed the same time as when he started to climb the coloured scarf.

Hearing his mother's footsteps outside his door, he sprang back into bed and pretended to be asleep. The door opened.

Mother came into his room with a big parcel. In spite of the gay Christmas paper it was obvious it was a blackboard and easel. She crept quietly out again and Hugo watched through one half open eye.

It was a beautiful blackboard. Hugo knew where it had come from because there was a picture of Santa drawn on it with white chalk. As he hugged his easel, he noticed another tiny parcel. Opening it up he found a box of coloured chalks.

Written on the label, in very bad spelling, was:

CoRY about the MICKs up.
    The Eester ßunnys